The Crescent Moon

EX-LIBRIS

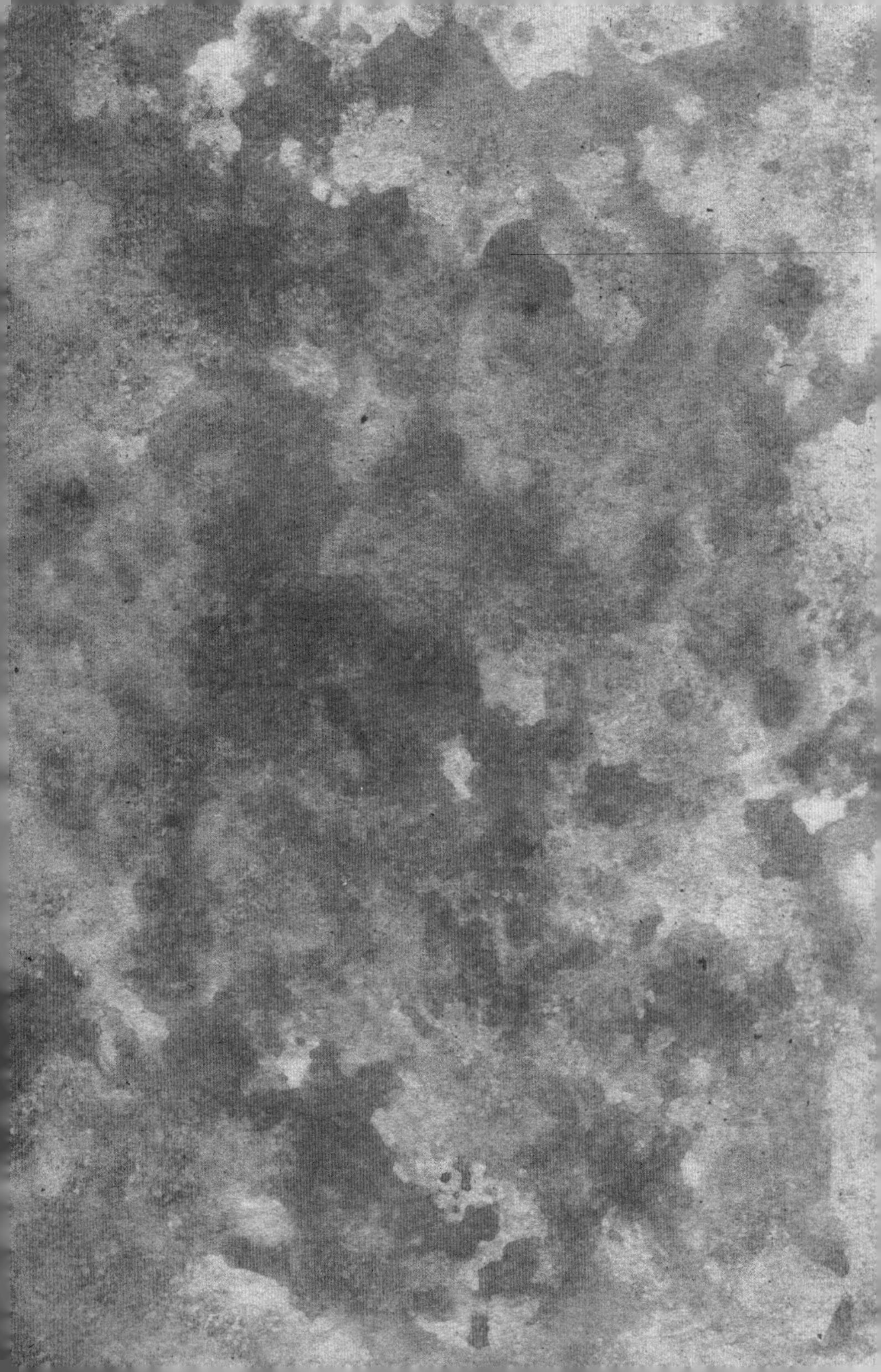

新月集

泰戈爾詩選/

中英對照雙語版

The Crescent Moon

泰戈爾——著
鄭振鐸——譯

笛藤出版

前言

唯美詩化的文字，猶如夜幕蒼穹中的密佈星羅，自悠久的歷史長河之中散發出璀璨迷人的耀目光環，是人類精神世界中無價的瑰寶。千百年來，由各種文字所組成的篇章，經由傳遞淬煉，使其在各種文學彙集而成的花園中不斷綻放出絢幻之花，讓人們沉浸於美好的閱讀時光。

作者們以凝練的語言、鮮明的節奏，反映著世界萬象的生活樣貌，並以各種形式向世人展現他們內心豐富多彩的情感世界。每個民族、地域的文化都有其精妙之處，西洋文學往往直接抒發作者的思想，愛、自由、和平，言盡而意亦盡，毫無造作之感。

18～19世紀，西洋文學的發展進入彰顯浪漫主義色彩的時期。所謂浪漫主義，就是用熱情奔放的言辭、絢麗多彩的想像與直白誇飾的表現手法，直接抒發出作者對理想世界熱切追求與渴望的情感。《世界經典文學 中英對照》系列，精選了浪漫主義時期一些作者們的代表作，包括泰戈爾的《新月集》、《漂鳥集》；雪萊的《西風頌》；濟慈的《夜鶯頌》；拜倫的《漫步在美的光影》；葉慈的《塵世玫瑰》。讓喜文之人盡情地徜徉於優美的字裡行間，領略作者及作品的無盡風采，享受藝術與美的洗禮。本系列所精選出的作品在世界文學領域中皆為經典名作，因此特別附上英文，方便讀者對照賞析英文詩意之美，並可同時提升英文閱讀與寫作素養。

在這一系列叢書當中，有對自然的禮讚，有對愛與和平的歌頌，有對孩童時代的讚美，也有對人生哲理的警示……，作者們在其一生中經歷了數次變革，以文字的形式寫下了無數天真、優美、現實、或悲哀的篇章，以無限的情懷吸引著所有各國藝文人士。文學界的名人郭沫若與冰心便是受到泰戈爾這位偉大詩人所著詩歌的影響，在一段時期內寫出了很多類似的詩作。在世界文學界諸多名人當中有貴族、政治名人、社會名流、也有普羅大眾，他們來自不同的國家、種族，無論一生平順或是坎坷，但其所創作品無一不是充滿了對世間的熱愛，對未來美好世界的無限嚮往。

編按：由於經過時間變遷、地域上的區別，許多遣辭用句也多所改變，為期望能更貼近現代讀者，本書以原譯與英文語意為基礎加以潤飾，希望讀者能以更貼近生活的語詞，欣賞泰戈爾所欲傳達的詩意哲理。

目　次 /

新月集。

The Crescent Moon

家庭／

我獨自走過阡陌之間，夕陽正掩藏起最後那道金色光芒，像個守財奴。

白晝逐漸深陷黑暗，收割後的田地，如寡婦般沉默不語。

突然，男孩的高亢歌聲劃破天際。他穿越看不見的黑暗，餘音迴盪在靜謐的夜晚。

他的鄉村屋舍座落在荒地盡頭，在甘蔗田後，隱藏在香蕉樹、細長的檳榔樹、椰子樹和深綠菠蘿蜜果樹的樹影裡。

我在星光下踽踽獨行，駐足片刻，看見黑暗的大地展開在我的眼前，用她的手臂擁抱著無數的家庭，那些家庭裡有著搖籃和床鋪，母親們的心和夜燈，還有年輕的生命，他們滿懷喜悅，卻渾然不知自己對於世界的價值。

The Home

I paced alone on the road across the field while the sunset was hiding its last gold like a miser.

The daylight sank deeper and deeper into the darkness, and the widowed land, whose harvest had been reaped, lay silent.

Suddenly a boy's shrill voice rose into the sky. He traversed the dark unseen, leaving the track of his song across the hush of the evening.

His village home lay there at the end of the waste land, beyond the sugar-cane field, hidden among the shadows of the banana and the slender areca palm, the cocoa-nut and the dark green jack-fruit trees.

I stopped for a moment in my lonely way under the starlight, and saw spread before me the darkened earth surrounding with her arms countless homes furnished with cradles and beds, mothers' hearts and evening lamps, and young lives glad with a gladness that knows nothing of its value for the world.

海濱／

孩子們聚集在無邊無際的海之濱。

頭上無垠的天空靜止不動，腳下的海水洶湧不息。孩子們聚集在無邊無際的海之濱，叫著、跳著。

他們用沙子造房，以貝殼嬉戲。把枯葉作成船，微笑地讓它們漂流在大海上。孩子們在世界的海邊，盡情嬉戲。

他們不知道怎樣游泳，他們不知道怎樣撒網。採珍珠的漁夫為了珍珠而潛水，商人在他們的船上航行，孩子們卻只是收集了小圓石，又將它們散落一地。他們不搜尋埋藏的寶藏；他們也不知道怎樣撒網。

大海笑著湧起波浪，而海灘的微笑蕩漾著粼粼波光。澎湃凶險的浪濤，對孩子們隨意哼唱著歌，宛如母親推著孩子的搖籃時一樣。

On the Seashore

On the seashore of endless worlds children meet.

The infinite sky is motionless overhead and the restless water is boisterous. On the seashore of endless world the children meet with shouts and dances.

They build their houses with sand, and they play with empty shells. With withered leaves they weave their boats and smilingly float them on the vast deep. Children have their play on the seashore of world.

They know not how to swim, they know not how to cast nets. Pearl-fishers dive for pearls, merchants sail in their ships, while children gather pebbles and scatter them again. They seek not for hidden treasures, they know not how to cast nets.

The sea surges up with laughter, and pale gleams the smile of the sea-beach. Death-dealing waves sing meaningless ballads to the children, even like a mother while rocking her baby's cradle.

大海和孩子們一同嬉戲，而海灘的微笑蕩漾著粼粼波光。

孩子們聚集在無邊無際的海之濱。暴風雨在清朗無痕的天空中漫遊，船隻在平靜無跡的海面上失事，死亡伺機而動，孩子們卻在遊戲，在無邊無際的海之濱，孩子們盛大地聚集著。

The sea plays with children, and pale gleams the smile of the sea-beach.

On the seashore of endless world children meet. Tempest roams in the pathless sky, ships are wrecked in the trackless water, death is abroad and children play. On the seashore of endless world is the great meeting of children.

來源／

掠過孩子雙眼的睡眠 —有誰知道它從何處而來？是的，有個傳說，說它來自精靈村落，那林蔭之下隱約閃爍著螢火蟲的光芒，掛著兩朵羞怯迷人的蓓蕾。它便是由此出現，來輕吻孩子的雙眼。

孩子熟睡時，在他唇上浮現的一抹微笑—有誰知道它從何處降生？是的，有個傳說，說新月的淡淡光芒，輕觸到消逝中的秋季之雲，微笑便誕生在沐浴於朝露的夢境中—當孩子熟睡時，那抹微笑便在他的唇上浮現。

孩子的小手小腳綻放出甜蜜溫柔的清新氣息—有誰知道它在何處久藏著？是的，當母親還是一位少女的時候，它已在愛的溫柔與沉靜的神秘中，潛伏在她的心裡了— 而後，孩子的小手小腳綻放出甜蜜溫柔的清新氣息。

The Source

The sleep that flits on baby's eyes—does anybody know from where it comes? Yes, there is a rumour that it has its dwelling where, in the fairy village among shadows of the forest dimly lit with glow-worms, there hang two shy buds of enchantment. From there it comes to kiss baby's eyes.

The smile that flickers on baby's lips when he sleeps—does anybody know where it was born? Yes, there is a rumour that a young pale beam of a crescent moon touched the edge of a vanishing autumn cloud, and there the smile was first born in the dream of a dew-washed morning—the smile that flickers on baby's lips when he sleeps.

The sweet, soft freshness that blooms on baby's limbs—does anybody know where it was hidden so long? Yes, when the mother was a young girl it lay pervading her heart in tender and silent mystery of love—the sweet, soft freshness that has bloomed on baby's limbs.

孩童之道／

只要孩子願意，此時此刻他就可飛上天堂。

他之所以不離開我們，並非毫無緣故。

他愛把頭枕在母親懷中，無時不刻要看到她。

孩子知曉各種睿智話語，雖然少有世人理解。

他之所以從不說話，並非毫無緣故。

他唯一想做的事，就是學習從母親的唇間說出來的話。那就是為什麼他看起來是如此天真。

孩子原有成堆的黃金與珍珠，但他來到這個世界上，卻宛若乞丐。

他之所以偽裝，並非毫無緣故。

這個親愛的、裸身的小乞丐，之所以裝得全然無助，是想要乞求母親無盡的愛。

孩子在微小的新月之地上，了無牽絆。

他之所以放棄了自由，並非毫無緣故。

Baby's Way

If baby only wanted to, he could fly up to heaven this moment.

It is not for nothing that he does not leave us.

He loves to rest his head on mother's bosom, and cannot ever bear to lose sight of her.

Baby knows all manner of wise words, though few on earth can understand their meaning.

It is not for nothing that he never wants to speak.

The one thing he wants is to learn mother's words from mother's lips. That is why he looks so innocent.

Baby had a heap of gold and pearls, yet he came like a beggar on to this earth.

It is not for nothing he came in such a disguise.

This dear little naked mendicant pretends to be utterly helpless, so that he may beg for mother's wealth of love.

Baby was so free from every tie in the land of the tiny crescent moon.

It was not for nothing he gave up his freedom.

他知道在母親內心的一隅，藏著無窮的快樂，被她親愛的雙臂所擁抱，其甜美遠勝過自由。

孩子從不知道如何哭泣。他住在極樂之地。

他之所以流淚，並非毫無緣故。

雖然他藉著臉上可愛的笑容，牽引母親一心向他，他因細故發出的哭聲，卻也惹人又憐又愛。

He knows that there is room for endless joy in mother's little corner of a heart, and it is sweeter far than liberty to be caught and pressed in her dear arms.

Baby never knew how to cry. He dwelt in the land of perfect bliss.

It is not for nothing he has chosen to shed tears.

Though with the smile of his dear face he draws mother's yearning heart to him, yet his little cries over tiny troubles weave the double bond of pity and love.

不被留意的盛會／

啊，是誰將小罩衫染上顏色，我的孩子，還把小紅衫罩住你討喜的小手小腳？

一早你就到庭院來玩，跑得跌跌撞撞地。

但是，是誰將小罩衫染上色，我的孩子？

是什麼事讓你笑開懷，我的小寶貝？

媽媽站在門邊，微笑地望著你。

她拍著手，手鐲叮噹響，你拿著竹竿跳舞，就像個小牧童。

但是，是什麼事讓你笑開懷，我的小寶貝？

喔，小貪心，你雙手摟著媽媽的脖子，要索討些什麼？

喔，貪得無饜的心，你要我把整個世界從天上摘下來，像摘果那樣，放在你粉嫩的小小掌心上嗎？

喔，小貪心，你要索討些什麼？

風兒興高采烈地帶走了你踝鈴的叮噹聲。

太陽微笑望著你梳洗。

The Unheeded Pageant

Ah, who was it coloured that little frock, my child, and covered your sweet limbs with that little red tunic?

You have come out in the morning to play in the courtyard, tottering and tumbling as you run.

But who was it coloured that little frock, my child?

What is it makes you laugh, my little life-bud?

Mother smiles at you standing on the threshold.

She claps her hands and her bracelets jingle, and you dance with your bamboo stick in your hand like a tiny little shepherd.

But what is it makes you laugh, my little life-bud?

O beggar, what do you beg for, clinging to your mother's neck with both your hands?

O greedy heart, shall I pluck the world like a fruit from the sky to place it on your little rosy palm?

O beggar, what are you begging for?

The wind carries away in glee the tinkling of your anklet bells.

The sun smiles and watches your toilet.

當你睡在媽媽的臂彎裡時，天空看顧你，而早晨躡手躡腳地走到你的床前，輕吻你的雙眼。

風兒興高采烈地帶走了你踝鈴的叮噹聲。

夢中的仙子穿過朦朧的天空，朝你飛來呢。

在你媽媽的心中，世界之母正坐在你身旁。

他，向星星奏樂的人，正拿著橫笛站在你的窗邊。

夢中的仙子穿過朦朧的天空，朝你飛來呢。

The sky watches over you when you sleep in your mother's arms, and the morning comes tiptoe to your bed and kisses your eyes.

The wind carries away in glee the tinkling of your anklet bells.

The fairy mistress of dreams is coming towards you, flying through the twilight sky.

The world-mother keeps her seat by you in your mother's heart.

He who plays his music to the stars is standing at your window with his flute.

And the fairy mistress of dreams is coming towards you, flying through the twilight sky.

睡眠小偷／

是誰從孩子的眼裡偷走了睡眠呢？我一定要知道。

媽媽把水罐緊靠著腰間，到村子附近取水。

正午時分。孩子們遊戲時間結束；池中的鴨子也靜默無聲。

牧童躺在榕樹的樹蔭下睡著了。

白鶴莊重而安靜地站在芒果樹叢旁的沼澤裡。

這個時候，睡眠小偷跑來，把睡眠從孩子的眼裡竊出，然後飛走。

媽媽回來時，看到孩子在屋子裡爬來爬去。

是誰從我們的孩子眼裡偷走了睡眠呢？我一定要找到她，把她鎖起來。

我一定要向那個黑洞裡張望，那裡有一道涓涓細流，流過巨石和石堆。

我一定要到醉花林中沉寂的樹影裡搜尋，鴿子在遠處咕咕叫，仙子的腳環在靜謐的星夜裡叮噹作響。

Sleep-Stealer

Who stole sleep from baby's eyes? I must know.

Clasping her pitcher to her waist, mother went to fetch water from the village near by.

It was noon. The children's playtime was over ; the ducks in the pond were silent.

The shepherd boy lay asleep under the shadow of the banyan tree.

The crane stood grave and still in the swamp near the mango grove.

In the meanwhile the Sleep-stealer came and, snatching sleep from baby's eyes, flew away.

When mother came back she found baby travelling the room over on all fours.

Who stole sleep from our baby's eyes? I must know. I must find her and chain her up.

I must look into that dark cave, where, through boulders and scowling stones, trickles a tiny stream.

I must search in the drowsy shade of the bakula grove, where pigeons coo in their corner, and fairies' anklets tinkle in the stillness of starry nights.

黃昏時，我要向寂靜的竹林裡窺望，在林中，螢火蟲揮霍著他們的光明，不論遇見哪個生物，我都要問他：「誰能告訴我睡眠小偷住在哪裡？」

是誰從我們的孩子眼裡偷走了睡眠呢？

只要我能抓住她，一定會好好教訓她！

我要闖入她的巢穴，看她把偷來的所有睡眠藏在哪裡。

我要全都奪走，帶回家去。

我要把她的雙翼牢牢綁住，把她放在河岸邊，讓她拿一根蘆葦，在燈心草和睡蓮間釣魚玩樂。

黃昏時市集已歇，村童都坐在媽媽的膝上時，夜鳥會在她耳邊取笑道：「你現在還想偷誰的睡眠呢？」

In the evening I will peep into the whispering silence of the bamboo forest, where fireflies squander their light, and will ask every creature I meet, "Can anybody tell me where the Sleep-stealer lives?"

Who stole sleep from baby's eyes? I must know.

Shouldn't I give her a good lesson if I could only catch her!

I would raid her nest and see where she hoards all her stolen sleep.

I would plunder it all, and carry it home.

I would bind her two wings securely, set her on the bank of the river, and then let her play at fishing with a reed among the rushes and water-lilies.

When the marketing is over in the evening, and the village children sit in their mothers' laps, then the night birds will mockingly din her ears with:

"Whose sleep will you steal now?"

開始／

「我是從哪裡來的，你在哪裡把我撿起來的？」孩子問他的媽媽說。

她把孩子緊緊地抱在懷裡，半哭半笑地答道—

「你曾是我藏在心裡的願望，我的寶貝。

你曾是我孩童時代玩的娃娃；每天早晨我用泥土塑造神像，那時我一做再做的就是你的模樣。

你曾和我們的家庭守護神一同受到祭祀，當我敬神之時，也同時崇敬著你。

你是我此生的希望和愛，而且你也活在我母親的生命裡。

長久以來，你被養育在不朽精靈的膝上，祂是我們的一家之主。

當我還是個女孩，我的心如花瓣般綻放，你就像盤旋於上的花香。

你在我年輕的身體上溫柔地盛開，像日出前天空中的一道光芒。

The Beginning

"Where have I come from, where did you pick me up?" the baby asked its mother.

She answered half crying, half laughing, and clasping the baby to her breast,— "You were hidden in my heart as its desire, my darling.

You were in the dolls of my childhood's games; and when with clay I made the image of my god every morning, I made and unmade you then.

You were enshrined with our household deity, in his worship I worshipped you.

In all my hopes and my loves, in my life, in the life of my mother you have lived.

In the lap of the deathless Spirit who rules our home you have been nursed for ages.

When in girlhood my heart was opening its petals, you hovered as a fragrance about it.

Your tender softness bloomed in my youthful limbs, like a glow in thc sky before the sunrise.

天堂的第一寵兒，晨曦的孿生兄弟，你從世界的生命之泉落下，終於停泊在我的心頭。

當我凝視你的臉龐，神秘之感湧向我；你原是屬於一切的，現在竟為我所有。

為了怕失去你，我把你緊緊地抱在懷裡。是怎樣的魔力把這稀世珍寶帶到我纖瘦的雙臂中呢？」

Heaven's first darling, twin-born with the morning light, you have floated down the stream of the world's life, and at last you have stranded on my heart.

As I gaze on your face, mystery overwhelms me; you who belong to all have become mine.

For fear of losing you I hold you tight to my breast. What magic has snared the world's treasure in these slender arms of mine?"

孩子的世界／

我願能在我孩子的世界裡，擁有一個安靜的小角落。

我知道星星會陪他說話，天空也會彎下腰，用傻氣的雲朵和彩虹來討好他。

那些裝傻、看起來不能走動的人，帶著故事，捧著盛滿絢麗玩具的托盤，蹣跚地來到他的窗前。

我願我能在孩子心中的道路行走，拋開一切的束縛；

在那裡，使者毫無理由地，為沒有歷史的諸王，奔走於國境之中；

在那裡，理智將她的律法做成風箏，放行天際，真理也讓事實掙脫桎梏，重獲自由。

Baby's World

I wish I could take a quiet corner in the heart of my baby's very own world.

I know it has stars that talk to him, and a sky that stoops down to his face to amuse him with its silly clouds and rainbows.

Those who make believe to be dumb, and look as if they never could move, come creeping to his window with their stories and with trays crowded with bright toys.

I wish I could travel by the road that crosses baby's mind, and out beyond all bounds;

Where messengers run errands for no cause between the kingdoms of kings of no history;

Where Reason makes kites of her laws and flies them, and Truth sets Fact free from its fetters.

當此之時，我便明白／

當我給你五顏六色的玩具時，我的孩子，我便明白為什麼雲朵和水面如此繽紛，為什麼花朵會染上絢爛的色彩—當我給你五顏六色的玩具時，我的孩子。

當我歌唱使你跳舞時，我真的知道為什麼樹葉會沙沙作響，為什麼波濤要將合奏的樂聲傳進默默聆聽的大地心上—當我歌唱而使你跳舞時。

當我把糖果放在你貪心的小手時，我知道為什麼花萼裡會有花蜜，為什麼果實會偷偷地滿溢甜美的汁液—當我把糖果放在你貪心的小手時。

當我親吻你的臉頰逗你微笑時，我的寶貝，我確實明白了晨光從空中流瀉而下時，是何等的愉悅，而夏天的微風吹拂在身上又是何等的舒爽—當我親吻你的臉頰逗你微笑時。

When and Why

When I bring you coloured toys, my child, I understand why there is such a play of colours on clouds, on water, and why flowers are painted in tints—when I give coloured toys to you, my child.

When I sing to make you dance, I truly know why there is music in leaves, and why waves send their chorus of voices to the heart of the listening earth—when I sing to make you dance.

When I bring sweet things to your greedy hands, I know why there is honey in the cup of the flower, and why fruits are secretly filled with sweet juice—when I bring sweet things to your greedy hands.

When I kiss your face to make you smile, my darling, I surely understand what pleasure streams from the sky in morning light, and what delight the summer breeze brings to my body—when I kiss you to make you smile.

責備／

為什麼你眼中有淚，我的孩子？

他們真是可怕，總是莫名其妙地責備你！

你寫字時墨水沾滿了手指和臉—他們因此嫌你髒嗎？

噢，呸！如果滿月的臉上也沾了墨水，他們膽敢嫌它髒嗎？

他們總是因為小事而責備你，我的孩子。他們隨時都想無中生有般地挑錯。

你玩耍時把衣服扯破了—他們因此說你不整潔嗎？

噢，呸！當秋之晨從襤褸的雲衣中露出微笑，他們又會怎麼說呢？

不用把他們所說的放在心上，我的孩子。

他們把你做錯的事列了張長長的清單。誰都知道你有多喜歡甜美的東西—他們因此說你貪心嗎？

噢，呸！對我們這些愛你的人，他們又會怎麼說呢？

Defamation

Why are those tears in your eyes, my child?

How horrid of them to be always scolding you for nothing?

You have stained your fingers and face with ink while writing—is that why they call you dirty?

O, fie! Would they dare to call the full moon dirty because it has smudged its face with ink?

For every little trifle they blame you, my child. They are ready to find fault for nothing.

You tore your clothes while playing—is that why they call you untidy?

O, fie! What would they call an autumn morning that smiles through its ragged clouds?

Take no heed of what they say to you, my child.

They make a long list of your misdeeds. Everybody knows how you love sweet things—is that why they call you greedy?

O, fie! What then would they call us who love you?

法官／

你想說他什麼儘管說吧，但是我知道我孩子的短處。

我並不是因為他完美才愛他，我愛他是因為他是我的小小孩。

如果你試著計較衡量他的優缺點，要怎麼知道他有多可愛呢？

當我必須處罰他的時候，他更是我生命的一部分了。

當我讓他流淚時，我的心也跟著他哭了。

只有我有權利責罰他，因為只有真正愛著他的人才會懲罰他。

The Judge

Say of him what you please, but I know my child's failings.

I do not love him because he is good, but because he is my little child.

How should you know how dear he can be when you try to weigh his merits against his faults.

When I must punish him he becomes all the more a part of my being.

When I cause his tears to come my heart weeps with him.

I alone have a right to blame and punish, for he only may chastise who loves.

玩具／

孩子，你坐在塵土上，整個早晨玩著斷掉的樹枝，是多麼開心呀。

我微笑地看你玩著那根斷掉的樹枝。

我正忙著記帳，幾個小時過去了，持續把數字疊疊加加。

也許你看著我心想：「這個遊戲好無聊，你竟然浪費了一個早上的時間！」

孩子，我已經忘了要怎麼專注把玩樹枝與泥塊了。

我尋求貴重的玩具，收集金塊與銀塊。

你無論找到什麼東西，都能創造出愉快的遊戲，我卻把時間與力氣都浪費在那些永遠無法得到的事物上。

我在脆弱的獨木舟裡，掙扎著要越過慾望之海，卻忘了自己也只是在玩遊戲而已。

Playthings

Child, how happy you are sitting in the dust, playing with a broken twig all the morning.

I smile at your play with that little bit of a broken twig.

I am busy with my accounts, adding up figures by the hour.

Perhaps you glance at me and think, "What a stupid game to spoil your morning with!"

Child, I have forgotten the art of being absorbed in sticks and mud-pies.

I seek out costly playthings, and gather lumps of gold and silver.

With whatever you find you create your glad games, I spend both my time and my strength over things I never can obtain.

In my frail canoe I struggle to cross the sea of desire, and forget that I too am playing a game.

天文家／

我只不過說，「當傍晚圓圓的滿月掛在迦曇波[1]的枝頭時，有人能去抓住它嗎？」

哥哥卻笑我說：「孩子呀，你真是我所見到最傻的孩子。月亮離我們這麼遠，誰能抓住它呢？」

我說，「哥哥，你真傻！當媽媽往窗外探頭，微笑著往下看我們玩遊戲時，你會說她遠嗎？」

哥哥還是說：「你真的是個傻孩子！但是，孩子，你要到哪裡去找一個大到能抓住月亮的網子呢？」

我說：「你當然可以用雙手去抓呀。」

但是哥哥還是笑我說：「你真是我所見到最傻的孩子！如果月亮靠過來，你就知道它有多大了。」

我說，「哥哥，你們學校裡所教的，真是沒有用呀！當媽媽低下頭親吻我們的時候，她的臉看起來有很大嗎？」

但是哥哥還是說，「你真是個傻孩子。」

[1] 迦曇波，原名 Kadam，亦作 Kadamba，學名 Namlea Cadamba，意譯「白花」，即曇花。

The Astronomer

I only said, "When in the evening the round full moon gets entangled among the branches of that Kadam tree, couldn't somebody catch it?"

But dada [elder brother] laughed at me and said, "Baby, you are the silliest child I have ever known. The moon is ever so far from us, how could anybody catch it?"

I said, "Dada how foolish you are! When mother looks out of her window and smiles down at us playing, would you call her far away?"

Still dada said, "You are a stupid child! But, baby, where could you find a net big enough to catch the moon with?"

I said, "Surely you could catch it with your hands."

But dada laughed and said, "You are the silliest child I have known. If it came nearer, you would see how big the moon is."

I said, "Dada, what nonsense they teach at your school! When mother bends her face down to kiss us does her face look very big?"

But still dada says, "You are a stupid child."

雲朵與波浪／

媽媽，住在雲端的人對我喊道—

「我們從睡醒時開始玩，一直玩到白天結束吧。

我們和金黃色的曙光玩遊戲，也和銀白色的月亮玩遊戲。」

我問：「但是，我要怎麼上去你那邊呢？」

他們回答：「你來地球的邊緣，舉手朝向天空，就可以被接到雲端裡來了。」

「我媽媽在家裡等我呢，」我說，「我怎麼能離她而去呢？」

然後他們微笑，飄浮而去。

但是我知道有比這個更好的遊戲，媽媽。

我來做雲，你當月亮。

我用雙手遮住你，我們的屋頂就是藍天。

住在波浪上的人對我喊道—

「我們從早晨唱歌到晚上；我們不斷往前旅行，不知道身處何方。」

Clouds and Waves

Mother, the folk who live up in the clouds call out to me—

"We play from the time we wake till the day ends.

We play with the golden dawn, we play with the silver moon."

I ask, "But, how am I to get up to you?"

They answer, "Come to the edge of the earth, lift up your hands to the sky, and you will be taken up into the clouds."

"My mother is waiting for me at home," I say. "How can I leave her and come?"

Then they smile and float away.

But I know a nicer game than that, mother.

I shall be the cloud and you the moon.

I shall cover you with both my hands, and our house-top will be the blue sky.

The folk who live in the waves call out to me—

"We sing from morning till night; on and on we travel and know not where we pass."

我問：「但是，我要怎麼加入你們的隊伍裡呢？」

他們說：「你站在岸邊，緊閉雙眼，就會被帶到波浪上來了。」

我說：「我媽媽要我在傍晚時回家—我怎麼能離她而去呢？」

然後他們微笑，舞動般流逝。

但是我知道有比這個更好的遊戲。

我當波浪，你當陌生的海岸。

我不斷滾動，笑著撞在你的腿上。

世界上就沒有人知道我們身處何方。

I ask, "But, how am I to join you?"

They tell me, "Come to the edge of the shore and stand with your eyes tight shut, and you will be carried out upon the waves."

I say, "My mother always wants me at home in the evening—how can I leave her and go?"

Then they smile, dance and pass by.

But I know a better game than that.

I will be the waves and you will be a strange shore.

I shall roll on and on and on, and break upon your lap with laughter.

And no one in the world will know where we both are.

金黃花／

假如我變成一朵金黃花[1]，只是為了好玩，長在高高的樹枝上，笑嘻嘻地在風中搖擺，又在新生的樹葉上跳舞，媽媽，你會認得我嗎？

你要是喊道，「孩子，你在哪裡呀？」我會暗自偷笑，保持安靜。

我會悄悄地綻放花瓣，看著你工作。

當你沐浴後，濕潤的秀髮散落肩上，穿過金黃花的林蔭，走到禱告的小庭院時，你會聞到花香，卻不知道這香味是從我飄散而來。

午餐後，你坐在窗前讀《羅摩衍那》[2]，當樹影落在你的髮稍與膝上時，我會把自己小小的影子投射在你的書頁上，剛好落在你讀到的地方。

[1] 金色花，原名 Champa，亦作 Champak，學名 Michelia Champaca，印度聖樹，木蘭花屬植物，開金黃色碎花，俗稱「黃玉蘭」。譯名亦做「瞻波伽」或「占波伽」。

[2] 《羅摩衍那（Ramayana）》為印度敘事詩，相傳為蟻垤（Valmiki）所作。今傳本形式約為公元二世紀間所形成。全書分為七卷，共二萬四千頌，皆為敘述羅摩生平之作。羅摩即羅摩犍陀羅，十車王之子，悉多之夫。他於第二世（Treta yaga）入世，為毗濕奴神第七化身。印人視他為英雄，亦有人崇拜如神。

The Champa Flower

Supposing I became a champa flower, just for fun, and grew on a branch high up that tree, and shook in the wind with laughter and danced upon the newly budded leaves, would you know me, mother?

You would call, "Baby, where are you?" and I should laugh to myself and keep quite quiet.

I should slyly open my petals and watch you at your work.

When after your bath, with wet hair spread on your shoulders, you walked through the shadow of the champa tree to the little court where you say your prayers, you would notice the scent of the flower, but not know that it came from me.

When after the midday meal you sat at the window reading Ramayana , and the tree's shadow fell over your hair and your lap, I should fling my wee little shadow on to the page of your book, just where you were reading.

但是你會猜得到，這就是你孩子的小影子嗎？

黃昏時當你拿著燈走進牛棚，我會轉瞬回歸塵世，再度成為你的孩子，求你講個故事給我聽。

「你到哪裡去了，你這個調皮的孩子？」

「我不告訴你，媽媽。」這將是那時我們之間的對話了。

But would you guess that it was the tiny shadow of your little child?

When in the evening you went to the cow-shed with the lighted lamp in your hand, I should suddenly drop on to the earth again and be your own baby once more, and beg you to tell me a story.

"Where have you been, you naughty child?"

"I won't tell you, mother." That's what you and I would say then.

仙境／

如果人們知道了我的國王宮殿在哪裡，它就會消失無蹤。

在那裡白銀為牆，屋頂是耀眼的黃金。

皇后住在有七個庭院的宮殿裡；她戴的一串珠寶，等同於七個王國的所有財富。

不過，讓我小小聲地告訴你，媽媽，我的國王宮殿究竟在哪裡。

它就在我們陽臺角落，在那種著杜爾茜花的花盆那邊。

公主躺在岸上沉睡著，遠遠地隔著七座無法跨越的海洋。

除了我以外，世上無人能夠找到她。

她手戴鐲子，耳垂上掛著珍珠；髮長及地。

Fairyland

If people came to know where my king's palace is, it would vanish into the air.

The walls are of white silver and the roof of shining gold.

The queen lives in a palace with seven courtyards, and she wears a jewel that cost all the wealth of seven kingdoms.

But let me tell you, mother, in a whisper, where my king's palace is.

It is at the corner of our terrace where the pot of the tulsi plant stands.

The princess lies sleeping on the far-away shore of the seven impassable seas.

There is none in the world who can find her but myself.

She has bracelets on her arms and pearl drops in her ears; her hair sweeps down upon the floor.

當我用魔杖輕觸她時，她就會醒過來，而當她微笑時，珍珠將會從她唇邊滾落。

不過，讓我在你耳邊小小聲地告訴你，媽媽，她就住在我們陽臺角落，在那種著杜爾茜花的花盆那邊。

當你要到河邊沐浴時，走到屋頂的那座陽臺上吧。

我就坐在牆角陰影匯聚之處。

我只讓小貓跟我在一起，因為她知道故事裡的理髮匠住在哪裡。

不過，讓我在你耳邊小小聲地告訴你，故事裡的理髮匠到底住在哪裡。

他住的地方，就在陽臺角落，在那種著杜爾茜花的花盆那邊。

She will wake when I touch her with my magic wand, and jewels will fall from her lips when she smiles.

But let me whisper in your ear, mother; she is there in the corner of our terrace where the pot of the tulsi plant stands.

When it is time for you to go to the river for your bath, step up to that terrace on the roof.

I sit in the corner where the shadows of the walls meet together.

Only puss is allowed to come with me, for she knows where the barber in the story lives.

But let me whisper, mother, in your ear where the barber in the story lives.

It is at the corner of the terrace where the pot of the tulsi plant stands.

流放之地／

媽媽，天色變灰暗了；我不知道現在幾點了。

我玩得不起勁，所以到你這裡來。今天星期六，是我們的休息日。

放下你的工作，媽媽，坐在窗邊，告訴我童話裡的特潘塔沙漠在什麼地方？

雨的陰影完全遮住了白天。

兇猛的閃電用爪子抓著天空。

當天上烏雲轟隆作響打雷，我內心害怕時，總愛爬到你的身上。

當大雨傾洩在竹葉上好幾個小時，而我們的窗戶被狂風震得格格作響時，我就愛獨自和你坐在屋裡，媽媽，聽你講童話裡的特潘塔沙漠。

它在哪裡，媽媽，在哪一個海洋的岸上，在哪座山腳下，在哪一位國王的國土裡？

The Land of the Exile

Mother, the light has grown grey in the sky; I do not know what the time is.

There is no fun in my play, so I have come to you. It is Saturday, our holiday.

Leave off your work, mother; sit here by the window and tell me where the desert of Tepantar in the fairy tale is?

The shadow of the rains has covered the day from end to end.

The fierce lightning is scratching the sky with its nails.

When the clouds rumble and it thunders, I love to be afraid in my heart and cling to you.

When the heavy rain patters for hours on the bamboo leaves, and our windows shake and rattle at the gusts of wind, I like to sit alone in the room, mother, with you, and hear you talk about the desert of Tepantar in the fairy tale.

Where is it, mother, on the shore of what sea, at the foot of what hills, in the kingdom of what king?

田野上沒有圍籬的界線，也沒有村人在黃昏時走過的足跡，或是婦人在樹林裡檢拾枯枝而捆載到市場去的道路。沙地上只有小塊的黃色草地，只有一棵樹，樹上有一對聰明的成鳥在那裡築巢，而那裡就是特潘塔沙漠。

我能夠想像，在這樣烏雲密佈的天氣，國王的小兒子如何獨自騎著灰馬橫渡沙漠，尋找在不可知的重洋之外，被囚禁在巨人宮殿裡的公主。

當雨霧在遠處的天空落下，閃電像一陣突然發作的痛楚四射時，他是否還記得他不幸的母親，被國王拋棄，一邊掃除牛棚，一邊拭淚，當他騎馬走過童話裡的特潘塔沙漠時？

看，媽媽，日子還沒結束天就黑了，也沒有什麼旅客走在那邊村莊的路上。

牧童早已從牧場返家，人們都已從田裡回來，坐在茅屋屋簷下的草席，看著陰暗的雲朵。

There are no hedges there to mark the fields, no footpath across it by which the villagers reach their village in the evening, or the woman who gathers dry sticks in the forest can bring her load to the market. With patches of yellow grass in the sand and only one tree where the pair of wise old birds have their nest, lies the desert of Tepantar.

I can imagine how, on just such a cloudy day, the young son of the king is riding alone on a grey horse through the desert, in search of the princess who lies imprisoned in the giant's palace across that unknown water.

When the haze of the rain comes down in the distant sky, and lightning starts up like a sudden fit of pain, does he remember his unhappy mother, abandoned by the king, sweeping the cow-stall and wiping her eyes, while he rides through the desert of Tepantar in the fairy tale?

See, mother, it is almost dark before the day is over, and there are no travellers yonder on the village road.

The shepherd boy has gone home early from the pasture, and men have left their fields to sit on mats under the eaves of their huts, watching the scowling clouds.

媽媽，我把所有的書都放在書架上了—現在不要叫我做功課。

當我長得像爸爸一樣大時，我會學到一切必要的知識。

但是今天，你得告訴我，媽媽，童話裡的特潘塔沙漠在什麼地方？

Mother, I have left all my books on the shelf—do not ask me to do my lessons now.

When I grow up and am big like my father, I shall learn all that must be learnt.

But just for to-day, tell me, mother, where the desert of Tepantar in the fairy tale is?

雨天／

烏雲快速聚集在森林漆黑的外圍。

噢，孩子，不要出去呀！

湖邊的一排棕櫚樹，擺著頭撞向陰暗的天空；羽毛凌亂的烏鴉，安靜地棲息在羅望子樹枝上，河的東岸逐漸被加深的黑暗所包圍。

我們的牛繫在籬上，高聲鳴叫。

噢，孩子，在這裡等著，等我把牛牽進牛棚裡。

人們都擠在淹水的田裡，捕捉從滿溢的池塘中逃出來的魚兒，雨水成了小河，流過狹窄的巷弄，像一個嬉笑的孩子，從媽媽那裡跑走，故意戲弄她。

聽呀，有人在淺灘上呼喊船夫。

噢，孩子，天色暗了，渡船頭的船已經停了。

The Rainy Day

Sullen clouds are gathering fast over the black fringe of the forest.

O child, do not go out!

The palm trees in a row by the lake are smiting their heads against the dismal sky; the crows with their draggled wings are silent on the tamarind branches, and the eastern bank of the river is haunted by a deepening gloom.

Our cow is lowing loud, tied at the fence.

O child, wait here till I bring her into the stall.

Men have crowded into the flooded field to catch the fishes as they escape from the overflowing ponds; the rain water is running in rills through the narrow lanes like a laughing boy who has run away from his mother to tease her.

Listen, someone is shouting for the boatman at the ford.

O child, the daylight is dim, and the crossing at the ferry is closed.

天空彷彿在滂沱的雨上快跑著；河裡的水吵鬧而不耐煩；婦人們早已拿著汲滿水的水罐，從恆河畔匆匆地回家了。

必須準備好夜裡用的燈。

噢，孩子，不要出去呀！

往市場的路已無人煙，到河邊的路濕滑不已。風在竹林裡咆哮，有如困在網中的野獸般極力掙扎。

The sky seems to ride fast upon the madly-rushing rain; the water in the river is loud and impatient; women have hastened home early from the Ganges with their filled pitchers.

The evening lamps must be made ready.

O child, do not go out!

The road to the market is desolate, the lane to the river is slippery. The wind is roaring and struggling among the bamboo branches like a wild beast tangled in a net.

紙船／

日復一日，我將一艘艘紙船放進潺潺溪流中。

我把自己和村子的名字，用黑筆大大地寫在紙船上。

我希望某個住在異地的人會找到紙船並且認識我。

我把花園裡的秀利花放進小船上，希望這些黎明綻放的花朵能在夜裡順利上岸。

我將紙船放到河裡，仰望天空，看見小小雲朵宛如滿帆。

我不知道天空中有哪個玩伴把這些船放下來跟我的船比賽！

夜晚降臨，我的臉埋在手臂裡，夢見我的紙船在子夜的星光下載浮載沉。

睡夢仙子駕著一艘艘船，他們的籃子裡滿載夢境。

Paper Boats

Day by day I float my paper boats one by one down the running stream.

In big black letters I write my name on them and the name of the village where I live.

I hope that someone in some strange land will find them and know who I am.

I load my little boats with shiuli flowers from our garden, and hope that these blooms of the dawn will be carried safely to land in the night.

I launch my paper boats and look up into the sky and see the little clouds setting their white bulging sails.

I know not what playmate of mine in the sky sends them down the air to race with my boats!

When night comes I bury my face in my arms and dream that my paper boats float on and on under the midnight stars.

The fairies of sleep are sailing in them, and the lading is their baskets full of dreams.

水手／

船夫曼特胡的船隻停泊在拉琪根琪碼頭。

這艘船雖然載著黃麻，但卻無用地閒置已久。

只要他願意把船借給我，我會裝上一百隻槳，揚起五、六、七張帆。

我絕不會將船開到愚蠢的市集。

我將航遍仙境裡的七座大海和十三條河道。

但是，媽媽，你不會躲在角落為我哭泣。

我不會像羅摩犍陀羅 [1] 那樣跑進森林裡，十四年才回來。

我會成為故事中的王子，讓船滿載我心所喜。

我將帶我的朋友阿蘇和我做伴，我們要快樂地在仙境裡的七座大海和十三條河道裡航行。

我們會在晨曦中揚帆起航。

The Sailor

The boat of the boatman Madhu is moored at the wharf of Rajgunj.

It is uselessly laden with jute, and has been lying there idle for ever so long.

If he would only lend me his boat, I should man her with a hundred oars, and hoist sails, five or six or seven.

I should never steer her to stupid markets.

I should sail the seven seas and the thirteen rivers of fairyland.

But, mother, you won't weep for me in a corner.

I am not going into the forest like Ramachandra to come back only after fourteen years.

I shall become the prince of the story, and fill my boat with whatever I like.

I shall take my friend Ashu with me. We shall sail merrily across the seven seas and the thirteen rivers of fairyland.

We shall set sail in the early morning light.

午間當你在池中沐浴時，我們應該已身在陌生的國度。

我們將經過特浦尼淺灘，越過特潘塔沙漠。

我們會在夜幕降臨時回來，我將娓娓道來我們的所見所聞。

我將穿越仙境裡的七座大海和十三條河道。

[1] 羅摩犍陀羅即羅摩。他是印度敘事詩《羅摩衍那》中的主角。為了尊重父親的諾言和維持弟兄間的友愛，他拋棄了繼承王位的權利，和妻子悉多在森林中被放逐了十四年。

When at noontide you are bathing at the pond, we shall be in the land of a strange king.

We shall pass the ford of Tirpurni, and leave behind us the desert of Tepantar.

When we come back it will be getting dark, and I shall tell you of all that we have seen.

I shall cross the seven seas and the thirteen rivers of fairyland.

對岸／

我渴望能到河的對岸去。

在那邊，船隻排成一列繫在竹竿上；

早晨，人們乘船到對岸去，肩上扛著犁，要去耕耘遠處的田地；

在那邊，牧人讓他們哞叫著的牛隻，游泳到河旁的牧場去；

傍晚他們都回家了，只留下豺狼在這長滿野草的島上嚎叫。

媽媽，如果你不介意，我長大以後，要做這渡口的船夫。

據說有些古怪的池塘藏在高處的河岸後面。

下過雨後，成群的野鴨飛到那裡，茂盛的蘆葦沿著岸邊生長，水鳥在那裡下蛋；

竹雞的尾巴隨之起舞，並將細小的足跡印在潔淨的軟泥上；

The Further Bank

I long to go over there to the further bank of the river,

Where those boats are tied to the bamboo poles in a line;

Where men cross over in their boats in the morning with ploughs on their shoulders to till their far-away fields;

Where the cowherds make their lowing cattle swim across to the riverside pasture;

Whence they all come back home in the evening, leaving the jackals to howl in the island overgrown with weeds,

Mother, if you don't mind, I should like to become the boatman of the ferry when I am grown up.

They say there are strange pools hidden behind that high bank,

Where flocks of wild ducks come when the rains are over, and thick reeds grow round the margins where waterbirds lay their eggs;

Where snipes with their dancing tails stamp their tiny footprints upon the clean soft mud;

黃昏時，高高的草叢頂著白花，邀月光在綠浪上滑行。

媽媽，如果你不介意，我長大以後，要做渡船的船夫。

我要橫越此岸到彼岸，村裡所有正在河中沐浴的男孩女孩，都會詫異地望著我。

當太陽升到日正當中，早晨變為正午，我將跑向你說道：「媽媽，我餓了！」

一天結束，影子縮到樹底下，我便要在黃昏中回到家裡。

我永遠不會像爸爸那樣，離開你到城裡工作。

媽媽，如果你不介意，我長大以後，要做這渡口的船夫。

Where in the evening the tall grasses crested with white flowers invite the moonbeam to float upon their waves.

Mother, if you don't mind, I should like to become the boatman of the ferryboat when I am grown up.

I shall cross and cross back from bank to bank, and all the boys and girls of the village will wonder at me while they are bathing.

When the sun climbs the mid sky and morning wears on to noon, I shall come running to you, saying, "Mother, I am hungry!"

When the day is done and the shadows cower under the trees, I shall come back in the dusk.

I shall never go away from you into the town to work like father.

Mother, if you don't mind, I should like to become the boatman of the ferryboat when I am grown up.

花的學校／

當暴風雨在空中轟隆作響，落下六月陣雨時，

潮濕的東風走過荒野，在竹林中吹著風笛。

於是花叢突然綻放，無人知曉來處，卻在綠草之上狂舞。

媽媽，我真心覺得那花叢在地底學校裡上學。

他們做功課時把門關上，如果他們想在時間到之前就跑出來玩，老師會罰他們站在牆角。

一旦下雨，他們就放假了。

樹枝在樹林裡互相碰觸，樹葉在狂風裡沙沙作響，雷雲大聲拍手，花孩子們便在那時候穿上粉紅的、黃的、白的衣裳，衝了出來。

你可知道，媽媽，他們的家在天上，在星星居住的地方。

The Flower-School

When storm clouds rumble in the sky and June showers come down,

The moist east wind comes marching over the heath to blow its bagpipes among the bamboos.

Then crowds of flowers come out of a sudden, from nobody knows where, and dance upon the grass in wild glee.

Mother, I really think the flowers go to school underground.

They do their lessons with doors shut, and if they want to come out to play before it is time, their master makes them stand in a corner.

When the rains come they have their holidays.

Branches clash together in the forest, and the leaves rustle in the wild wind, the thunder-clouds clap their giant hands and the flower children rush out in dresses of pink and yellow and white.

Do you know, mother, their home is in the sky, where the stars are.

你沒看見他們急著要到那裡去嗎？你不知道他們為什麼那樣匆忙嗎？

當然，我能猜到他們在對誰招手：他們也有媽媽，就像我一樣。

Haven't you seen how eager they are to get there? Don't you know why they are in such a hurry?

Of course, I can guess to whom they raise their arms: they have their mother as I have my own.

商人／

想像一下，媽媽，如果你待在家裡，而我到外地去旅行。

再想像，我的船已經滿載，準備啟航了。

現在，媽媽，好好想想再告訴我，回來的時候希望我帶些什麼給你。

媽媽，你想要成堆的黃金嗎？

在金河的兩岸，田野裡滿是金色的收成。

在林蔭小徑，金黃花散落滿地。

為了你，我要用幾百個籃子把花裝起來。

媽媽，你想要跟秋天的雨點一樣大的珍珠嗎？

我要渡海到珍珠島的岸邊。

在那裡的清晨曙光中，珍珠在草地上的野花裡顫動，珠子落在綠草上，被狂野的海浪大把大把地灑在沙灘上。

The Merchant

Imagine, mother, that you are to stay at home and I am to travel into strange lands.

Imagine that my boat is ready at the landing fully laden.

Now think well, mother, before you say what I shall bring for you when I come back.

Mother, do you want heaps and heaps of gold?

There, by the banks of golden streams, fields are full of golden harvest.

And in the shade of the forest path the golden champa flowers drop on the ground.

I will gather them all for you in many hundred baskets.

Mother, do you want pearls big as the raindrops of autumn?

I shall cross to the pearl island shore.

There in the early morning light pearls tremble on the meadow flowers, pearls drop on the grass, and pearls are scattered on the sand in spray by the wild sea-waves.

哥哥會得到一對有翅膀的馬，能帶他在雲端飛翔。

我要帶給爸爸一枝有魔力的筆，在他還來不及察覺的時候，筆就寫出字來了。

你呢，媽媽，我一定要把首飾箱和珠寶送給你，它們的價值可比七個國王的領土。

My brother shall have a pair of horses with wings to fly among the clouds.

For father I shall bring a magic pen that, without his knowing, will write of itself.

For you, mother, I must have the casket and jewel that cost seven kings their kingdoms.

同情／

如果我只是隻小狗，而不是你的小孩，親愛的媽媽，當我想吃你的盤裡的餐點時，你會對我說「不」嗎？

你會把我趕開，對我說：「走開，你這淘氣的小狗！」嗎？

那麼，走吧，媽媽，走吧！當你叫我時，我將永遠不過去，也不讓你餵我。

如果我只是隻綠色的小鸚鵡，而不是你的小孩，親愛的媽媽，你會把我鎖住，怕我飛走嗎？

你會搖手說道：「多麼不知感恩的鳥呀！整日整夜地在咬鏈子嗎？」

那麼，走吧，媽媽，走吧！我要跑到樹林裡去，永遠不讓你把我抱在懷裡了。

Sympathy

If I were only a little puppy, not your baby, mother dear, would you say "No" to me if I tried to eat from your dish?

Would you drive me off, saying to me,"Get away, you naughty little puppy?"

Then go, mother, go! I will never come to you when you call me, and never let you feed me any more.

If I were only a little green parrot, and not your baby, mother dear, would you keep me chained lest I should fly away?

Would you shake your finger at me and say, "What an ungrateful wretch of a bird! It is gnawing at its chain day and night?"

Then, go, mother, go! I will run away into the woods; I will never let you take me in your arms again.

職業／

早上當鐘敲了十響時，我會沿著小巷走去學校。

每天我都遇見那個小販，叫道：「鐲子，亮晶晶的鐲子！」

他沒有急著要做什麼，沒有一定要走哪條路，沒有一定得去哪裡，沒有一定哪時候回家。

我情願當一個小販，在街上過日子，叫著，「鐲子，亮晶晶的鐲子！」

下午四點，我從學校回家的時候。

我可以從家門看見一個園丁在花園裡掘地。

他隨心所欲地使用鋤頭，衣服被泥土弄髒，無論他被太陽曬黑了，或是身上被打濕了，都沒有人罵他。

我情願當一個園丁，在花園裡掘地。誰也不會來阻止我。

只是當傍晚天色一黑，媽媽要送我上床睡覺。

Vocation

When the gong sounds ten in the morning and I walk to school by our lane,

Every day I meet the hawker crying, "Bangles, crystal bangles!"

There is nothing to hurry him on, there is no road he must take, no place he must go to, no time when he must come home.

I wish I were a hawker, spending my day in the road, crying, "Bangles, crystal bangles!"

When at four in the afternoon I come back from the school.

I can see through the gate of that house the gardener digging the ground.

He does what he likes with his spade, he soils his clothes with dust, nobody takes him to task if he gets baked in the sun or gets wet.

I wish I were a gardener digging away at the garden with nobody to stop me from digging.

Just as it gets dark in the evening and my mother sends me to bed.

我可以從開著的窗戶，看見巡夜人走來走去。

小巷裡又黑又冷清，豎立的路燈彷彿是頭上長著紅眼睛的巨人。

巡夜人搖著他的提燈，跟著身邊的影子一起走著，他終生都沒有上床休息過。

我情願當一個巡夜人，整夜在街上走，提著燈去追逐影子。

I can see through my open window the watchman walking up and down.

The lane is dark and lonely, and the street-lamp stands like a giant with one red eye in its head.

The watchman swings his lantern and walks with his shadow at his side, and never once goes to bed in his life.

I wish I were a watchman walking the streets all night, chasing the shadows with my lantern.

長者／

媽媽，你的孩子真傻！她是那麼地幼稚不懂事！

她竟然不知道如何區分路燈和星星。

當我們玩著把小石子當食物的遊戲時，她真的以為它們是食物，竟想放進嘴裡去。

當我在她面前翻開一本書，要她讀 a、b、c 時，她卻用手把書撕了，突然高興地叫起來；你的孩子就是這樣做功課的。

當我生氣地對她搖頭，責備她頑皮時，她卻哈哈大笑，覺得很有趣。

誰都知道爸爸不在家，但是，如果我在遊戲時高叫一聲「爸爸」，她會高興地四處張望，以為爸爸就在附近。

當我把洗衣工帶來載衣服的驢子當學生，並且警告她說我是老師時，她卻會沒來由地亂叫起我哥哥來。

Superior

Mother, your baby is silly! She is so absurdly childish!

She does not know the difference between the lights in the streets and the stars.

When we play at eating with pebbles, she thinks they are real food, and tries to put them into her mouth.

When I open a book before her and ask her to learn her a, b, c, she tears the leaves with her hands and roars for joy at nothing; this is your baby's way of doing her lesson.

When I shake my head at her in anger and scold her and call her naughty, she laughs and thinks it great fun.

Everybody knows that father is away, but if in play I call aloud "Father," she looks about her in excitement and thinks that father is near.

When I hold my class with the donkeys that our washerman brings to carry away the clothes and I warn her that I am the schoolmaster, she will scream for no reason and call me dada (elder brother).

你的孩子想要捕捉月亮。她是這樣的好玩；把格尼許[1]叫成琪奴許。

媽媽，你的孩子真傻，她是那麼地幼稚不懂事！

[1] 格尼許（Ganesh）是毀滅之神濕婆的兒子，象頭人身。同時也是現代印度人最喜歡用來取名的首選。

Your baby wants to catch the moon. She is so funny; she calls Ganesh Ganush.

Mother, your baby is silly, she is so absurdly childish!

小大人／

我很小，因為我還是一個小孩。等我跟爸爸一樣大時，就是大人了。

我的老師要是走過來說：「很晚了，把你的石板和書拿來。」

我會告訴他：「你不知道我已經長得跟爸爸一樣大了嗎？我不要再做作業了。」

老師將會驚訝地說：「愛讀不讀隨便他，因為他已經長大了。」

我會自己穿上衣服，走進人潮擁擠的市場裡。

我的叔叔會跑過來說：「你會迷路的，我的孩子，讓我帶路吧。」

我會回答：「你沒有看見嗎，叔叔，我已經跟爸爸一樣大了。我要自己去市場。」

叔叔將會說：「是的，愛去哪裡隨便他，因為他已經長大了。」

我知道怎麼用鑰匙打開盒子，當我從盒子裡拿出錢給保姆時，媽媽會從浴室中出來。

The Little Big Man

I am small because I am a little child. I shall be big when I am as old as my father is.

My teacher will come and say, "It is late, bring your slate and your books."

I shall tell him, "Do you not know I am as big as father? And I must not have lessons any more."

My master will wonder and say, "He can leave his books if he likes, for he is grown up."

I shall dress myself and walk to the fair where the crowd is thick.

My uncle will come rushing up to me and say, "You will get lost, my boy; let me carry you."

I shall answer, "Can't you see, uncle, I am as big as father? I must go to the fair alone."

Uncle will say, "Yes, he can go wherever he likes, for he is grown up."

Mother will come from her bath when I am giving money to my nurse, for I shall know how to open the box with my key.

媽媽將會說：「你在做什麼呢，頑皮的孩子？」

我會告訴她：「媽媽，你不知道我已經跟爸爸一樣大了嗎？我必須拿錢給保姆。」

媽媽將會自言自語地說：「愛把錢給誰隨便他，因為他已經長大了。」

十月放假時爸爸將會回家，他會以為我還是一個小孩子，從城裡帶回小鞋子和小罩衫要給我。

我會說：「爸爸，把這些東西給哥哥吧，因為我已經跟你一樣大了。」

爸爸將會想一下，說道：「愛買什麼衣服隨便他，因為他已經長大了。」

Mother will say, "What are you about, naughty child?"

I shall tell her, "Mother, don't you know, I am as big as father, and I must give silver to my nurse."

Mother will say to herself, "He can give money to whom he likes, for he is grown up."

In the holiday time in October father will come home and, thinking that I am still a baby, will bring for me from the town little shoes and small silken frocks.

I shall say, "Father, give them to my dada [elder brother], for I am as big as you are."

Father will think and say, "He can buy his own clothes if he likes, for he is grown up."

十二點鐘／

媽媽，我現在真的不想做功課了。我整個早晨都在念書。

你說，現在只不過是十二點鐘。假如不會更晚；難道你不能把十二點鐘想像成下午嗎？

我能夠輕而易舉地想像：現在太陽已經曬到稻田的邊緣上了，年邁的漁婦正在池邊採香草做為晚餐。

我閉上了眼就能夠想像，馬塔爾樹下的陰影更黑了，池塘裡的水看起來黑得發亮。

假如十二點鐘能夠在黑夜裡降臨，為什麼黑夜不能在十二點鐘的時候現身呢？

The Twelve O'clock

Mother, I do want to leave off my lessons now. I have been at my book all the morning.

You say it is only twelve o'clock. Suppose it isn't any later; can't you ever think it is afternoon when it is only twelve o'clock?

I can easily imagine now that the sun has reached the edge of that rice-field, and the old fisher-woman is gathering herbs for her supper by the side of the pond.

I can just shut my eyes and think that the shadows are growing darker under the madar tree, and the water in the pond looks shiny black.

If twelve o'clock can come in the night, why can't the night come when it is twelve o'clock?

作家／

你說爸爸寫了許多書，但我卻不懂他所寫的東西。

整個傍晚他都在念書給你聽，但是你真的懂他的意思嗎？

媽媽，你講給我們聽的故事，真是好聽呀！我想不通，爸爸為什麼不能寫那樣的書呢？

難道他從來沒有從自己的媽媽那裡，聽過巨人、神仙和公主的故事嗎？

還是他已經完全忘記了？

他常常很晚才洗澡，你必須走過去，叫了一百多次他才來。

你等呀等，幫他熱菜，但他還寫著寫著，忘了一切。

爸爸總是把寫書當成玩遊戲。

如果我走進爸爸的房裡玩遊戲，你就會過來叫我：「真是一個頑皮的孩子！」

如果我稍微發出一點聲音，你就會說：「你沒有看見你爸爸正在工作嗎？」

寫呀寫的，有什麼樂趣呢？

Authorship

You say that father writes a lot of books, but what he writes I don't understand.

He was reading to you all the evening, but could you really make out what he meant?

What nice stories, mother, you can tell us! Why can't father write like that, I wonder?

Did he never hear from his own mother stories of giants and fairies and princesses?

Has he forgotten them all?

Often when he gets late for his bath you have to go and call him a hundred times.

You wait and keep his dishes warm for him, but he goes on writing and forgets.

Father always plays at making books.

If ever I go to play in father's room, you come and call me, "what a naughty child!"

If I make the slightest noise, you say, "Don't you see that father's at his work?"

What's the fun of always writing and writing?

當我拿起爸爸的鋼筆或鉛筆，像他那樣在書上寫著—a、b、c、d、e、f、g、h、i—為什麼那時候你會對我生氣呢，媽媽？

爸爸寫的時候，你卻從來不說一句話。

當我爸爸浪費了一大疊紙時，媽媽，你似乎毫不在意。

但是，如果我只拿了一張紙去做紙船，你就會說，「孩子，你真是在找麻煩！」

爸爸用黑色記號塗滿了一張張紙的正反面，你是怎樣想的呢？

When I take up father's pen or pencil and write upon his book just as he does,—a, b, c, d, e, f, g, h, i,—why do you get cross with me, then, mother?

You never say a word when father writes.

When my father wastes such heaps of paper, mother, you don't seem to mind at all.

But if I take only one sheet to make a boat with, you say, "Child, how troublesome you are!"

What do you think of father's spoiling sheets and sheets of paper with black marks all over on both sides?

壞郵差／

你為什麼坐在地上不發一語，告訴我，親愛的媽媽？

雨從開著的窗子打進來，你全身都濕透了，卻不在意。

你聽見鐘響了四下嗎？該是哥哥放學回家的時候了。

到底發生了什麼事，你的表情這麼奇怪？

你今天沒有接到爸爸的信嗎？

我看見郵差的袋子裝滿了信，幾乎鎮上的每個人都收到了。

只有爸爸的信，被他留下來自己看。我確定這個郵差是壞人。

但是不要因此傷心，親愛的媽媽。

明天是鄰村的市集，你叫女僕去買些紙筆。

我來寫爸爸要給你的信，而且你不會找出任何錯誤。

我會從 A 一直寫到 K。

The Wicked Postman

Why do you sit there on the floor so quiet and silent, tell me, mother dear?

The rain is coming in through the open window, making you all wet, and you don't mind it.

Do you hear the gong striking four? It is time for my brother to come home from school.

What has happened to you that you look so strange?

Haven't you got a letter from father today?

I saw the postman bringing letters in his bag for almost everybody in the town.

Only, father's letters he keeps to read himself. I am sure the postman is a wicked man.

But don't be unhappy about that, mother dear.

Tomorrow is market day in the next village. You ask your maid to buy some pens and papers.

I myself will write all father's letters; you will not find a single mistake.

I shall write from A right up to K.

但是，媽媽，為什麼你笑了呢？

你不相信我能寫得跟爸爸一樣好！

但是我將用心畫格子，把所有字母寫得又大又美。

當我寫好的時候，你以為我也像爸爸那麼傻，把信投入可怕的郵差袋裡嗎？

我會毫不遲疑地立刻送來給你，而且逐字地唸給你聽。

我知道那個郵差不會把真正很棒的信送給你。

But, mother, why do you smile?

You don't believe that I can write as nicely as father does!

But I shall rule my paper carefully, and write all the letters beautifully big.

When I finish my writing, do you think I shall be so foolish as father and drop it into the horrid postman's bag?

I shall bring it to you myself without waiting, and letter by letter help you to read my writing.

I know the postman does not like to give you the really nice letters.

英雄／

媽媽，想像一下我們正在旅行，經過一個陌生而危險的國度。

你坐在轎子裡，我騎著紅馬跑在你旁邊。

到了傍晚，太陽下山了。我們眼前的約拉地希的荒原疲乏而灰暗，大地淒涼而荒蕪。

你害怕地想—「我真不知道我們到哪裡了。」

我對你說：「媽媽，不要害怕。」

草地長遍針尖似的草，有條狹窄崎嶇的小徑穿梭其中。

廣袤的田野上看不見任何牛隻；牠們已經回到村裡的牛棚。

天色漸沉，大地和天空朦朧昏暗，我們無法辨別方向。

突然間你叫住我，小聲地問：「靠近河岸的是什麼火光呀？」

The Hero

Mother, let us imagine we are travelling, and passing through a strange and dangerous country.

You are riding in a palanquin and I am trotting by you on a red horse.

It is evening and the sun goes down. The waste of Joradighi lies wan and grey before us. The land is desolate and barren.

You are frightened and thinking—"I know not where we have come to."

I say to you, "Mother, do not be afraid."

The meadow is prickly with spiky grass, and through it runs a narrow broken path.

There are no cattle to be seen in the wide field; they have gone to their village stalls.

It grows dark and dim on the land and sky, and we cannot tell where we are going.

Suddenly you call me and ask me in a whisper, "What light is that near the bank?"

正在那時，傳出一陣可怕的尖叫，人影朝我們衝來。

你蹲在轎子裡，嘴裡喃喃地禱唸著神之名。

轎夫們嚇得發抖，躲藏在荊棘叢中。

我向你大喊：「不要害怕，媽媽，有我在這裡。」

他們手持長棍，披頭散髮，越走越近了。

我喊：「當心！你們這些壞蛋！再向前一步，你們就要送命了。」

他們又發出一陣可怕的吶喊聲，往前衝過來。

你抓住我的手，說道：「好孩子，看在上天的份上，躲開吧。」

我說：「媽媽，看我的。」

於是我策馬上前，猛奔過去，我的劍和盾彼此碰撞鏗鏘作響。

這場戰鬥令人畏懼，媽媽，如果你從轎子裡看得見的話，肯定會打冷顫的。

他們許多人逃走了，還有好些人被砍得支離破碎。

Just then there bursts out a fearful yell, and figures come running towards us.

You sit crouched in your palanquin and repeat the names of the gods in prayer.

The bearers, shaking in terror, hide themselves in the thorny bush.

I shout to you, "Don't be afraid, mother. I am here."

With long sticks in their hands and hair all wild about their heads, they come nearer and nearer.

I shout, "Have a care! You villains! One step more and you are dead men."

They give another terrible yell and rush forward.

You clutch my hand and say, "Dear boy, for heaven's sake, keep away from them."

I say, "Mother, just you watch me."

Then I spur my horse for a wild gallop, and my sword and buckler clash against each other.

The fight becomes so fearful, mother, that it would give you a cold shudder could you see it from your palanquin.

我知道你那時獨坐轎內，心裡想著，你的孩子這時候一定已經死了。

但是我跑到你面前，滿身是血，說道：「媽媽，戰鬥已經結束了。」

你走出來親吻我，擁我入懷，自言自語地說：

「如果沒有我的孩子護送我，我真不知道怎麼辦才好。」

每天都有一千件無用的事發生，為什麼這件事不能夠偶然實現呢？

這會很像書裡的故事。

我的哥哥會說：「這有可能嗎？我一直以為他很嬌弱呢！」

村裡的人們都會驚訝地說：「還好這孩子在媽媽身邊，簡直太幸運了！」

Many of them fly, and a great number are cut to pieces.

I know you are thinking, sitting all by yourself, that your boy must be dead by this time.

But I come to you all stained with blood, and say, "Mother, the fight is over now."

You come out and kiss me, pressing me to your heart, and you say to yourself,

"I don't know what I should do if I hadn't my boy to escort me."

A thousand useless things happen day after day, and why couldn't such a thing come true by chance?

It would be like a story in a book.

My brother would say, "Is it possible? I always thought he was so delicate!"

Our village people would all say in amazement, "Was it not lucky that the boy was with his mother?"

告別／

時候到了，媽媽，我走了。

昏暗孤寂的黎明時分，當你在黑暗中伸出雙臂，要擁抱睡在床上的孩子時，我會說：「孩子不在那裡！」—媽媽，我走了。

我要變成一股微風吹拂你；我要變成水中的漣漪，在你沐浴時一次次地親吻你。

夜裡一陣風吹，當雨點對著樹葉窸窸窣窣時，你躺在床上能聽見我的耳語，當閃電從開著的窗口打來時，我的笑聲也隨之閃進你的屋裡。

如果你醒著躺在床上，思念你的孩子直到深夜，我會從星空向你唱道：「睡呀！媽媽，睡呀。」

我要乘著每束迷路的月光，偷偷地來到你的床上，當你睡著時，躺在你的懷中。

我要變成一個夢，從你眼瞼的微縫中，溜進你的睡眠深處。當你醒來吃驚地張望時，我便如閃耀的螢火蟲般輕快地飛入黑暗中。

The End

It is time for me to go, mother; I am going.

When in the paling darkness of the lonely dawn you stretch out your arms for your baby in the bed, I shall say, "Baby is not there!"—mother, I am going.

I shall become a delicate draught of air and caress you; and I shall be ripples in the water when you bathe, and kiss you and kiss you again.

In the gusty night when the rain patters on the leaves you will hear my whisper in your bed, and my laughter will flash with the lightning through the open window into your room.

If you lie awake, thinking of your baby till late into the night, I shall sing to you from the stars, "Sleep mother, sleep."

On the straying moonbeams I shall steal over your bed, and lie upon your bosom while you sleep.

I shall become a dream, and through the little opening of your eyelids I shall slip into the depths of your sleep; and when you wake up and look round startled, like a twinkling firefly I shall flit out into the darkness.

在普耶大祭日[1]，當鄰居的孩子們來家裡玩時，我要融入笛聲裡，整天在你心頭迴盪。

親愛的阿姨帶了普耶禮[2]來，一定會問：「我們的孩子在哪裡，姊姊？」「媽媽，你要溫柔地告訴她：「他現在在我的瞳孔裡，在我的身體裡，在我的靈魂裡。」

[1] 普耶（Puja）意為「祭神大典」，這裡的「普耶大祭日」是指印度十月間的「難近母祭日」。

[2] 普耶禮就是指這個節日親友相互饋贈的禮物。

When, on the great festival of puja , the neighbours' children come and play about the house, I shall melt into the music of the flute and throb in your heart all day.

Dear auntie will come with puja -presents and will ask, "Where is our baby, sister?" Mother, you will tell her softly, "He is in the pupils of my eyes, he is in my body and in my soul."

召喚／

她離開時，夜色已黑，他們都睡了。

現在夜色亦黑，我向她呼喊：「回來，我的寶貝。世界都在沉睡，而星星彼此凝視，你悄悄過來一會兒，沒有人會知道的。」

她離開時，樹木正在萌芽，春光乍現。

現在花已盛開，我喊道：「回來，我的寶貝。孩子們漫不經心地遊戲，一會兒聚攏了花，一會兒又將花瓣散落各地。如果你來，帶走一朵小花，沒有人會發覺的。」

那些過去在玩遊戲的人，還在那裡玩樂，揮霍生命。

我聽著他們的空談，喊道：「回來，我的寶貝，媽媽的心裡充滿著愛，如果你來，從她那裡帶走一吻，沒有人會妒忌的。」

The Recall

The night was dark when she went away, and they slept.

The night is dark now, and I call for her, "Come back, my darling; the world is asleep; and no one would know, if you came for a moment while stars are gazing at stars."

She went away when the trees were in bud and the spring was young.

Now the flowers are in high bloom and I call, "Come back, my darling. The children gather and scatter flowers in reckless sport. And if you come and take one little blossom no one will miss it."

Those that used to play are pl-aying still, so spendthrift is life.

I listen to their chatter and call, "Come back, my darling, for mo-ther's heart is full to the brim with love, and if you come to snatch only one little kiss from her no one will grudge it."

初次的茉莉／

啊，這些茉莉花，這些潔白的茉莉花！

我依稀記得第一次雙手捧滿著茉莉花，這些潔白的茉莉花。

我喜愛陽光、天空，和翠綠的大地；

我聽見那河流淙淙的水聲，在黑漆的午夜裡傳來；

秋天的夕陽，在荒原的道路轉角迎接我，有如新娘揭起面紗迎接她的愛人。

當我想起孩提時第一次捧在手裡的白茉莉，心裡充滿著甜蜜的回憶。

我的一生中有過許多快樂的日子，在節慶宴會的夜裡，我曾跟著尋歡作樂者縱聲大笑。

在灰暗雨天的早晨，我低吟著許多飄逸的詩歌。

我的頸上戴著愛人手織的花環，作為晚裝。

當我想起孩提時第一次捧在手裡的白茉莉，心裡充滿著甜蜜的回憶。

The First Jasmines

Ah, these jasmines, these white jasmines!

I seem to remember the first day when I filled my hands with these jasmines, these white jasmines.

I have loved the sunlight, the sky and the green earth;

I have heard the liquid murmur of the river through the darkness of midnight;

Autumn sunsets have come to me at the bend of a road in the lonely waste, like a bride raising her veil to accept her lover.

Yet my memory is still sweet with the first white jasmines that I held in my hand when I was a child.

Many a glad day has come in my life, and I have laughed with merrym-akers on festival nights.

On grey mornings of rain I have crooned many an idle song.

I have worn round my neck the evening wreath of bakulas woven by the hand of love.

Yet my heart is sweet with the memory of the first fresh jasmines that filled my hands when I was a child.

榕樹／

喂，你，這個站在池畔亂糟糟的榕樹，你是否忘了那個小孩，就像你忘了曾在你的枝頭上築巢，卻又離開的鳥兒？

你難道不記得他怎樣坐在窗邊，驚奇地望著你深扎地下盤結的樹根嗎？

婦人們到池塘把水罐裝滿時，你龐大的黑影在水面上搖動，就像睡著的人掙扎著要醒來似的。

日光在水面的漣漪上跳舞，有如梭子不止息地在織著金色的織錦。

兩隻鴨子游在水草旁的倒影上，孩子靜坐沉思。

他渴望成為風，吹過你沙沙作響的樹枝；想成為你的影子，在水面上隨著日光而長；想成為鳥兒，棲息在你最高的枝枒上；他還想成為那兩隻鴨子，在蘆葦與影子間游來游去。

The Banyan Tree

O you shaggy-headed banyan tree standing on the bank of the pond, have you forgotten the little child, like the birds that have nested in your branches and left you?

Do you not remember how he sat at the window and wondered at the tangle of your roots that plunged underground?

The women would come to fill their jars in the pond, and your huge black shadow would wriggle on the water like sleep struggling to wake up.

Sunlight danced on the ripples like res-tless tiny shuttles weaving golden tapestry.

Two ducks swam by the weedy margin above their shadows, and the child would sit still and think.

He longed to be the wind and blow thr-ough your rustling branches, to be your sha-dow and lengthen with the day on the water, to be a bird and perch on your top-most twig, and to float like those ducks among the weeds and shadows.

祝福／

祝福這個小小心靈，這潔白的靈魂，已為我們的大地，贏得了上天一吻。

他熱愛日光，喜愛看見媽媽的臉龐。

他還不會睥睨塵土，渴求黃金。

將他抱在心口，並且祝福他。

他已來到這塊歧路百出的大地上了。

我不知道他如何從人海中選擇了你，來到你的門前，握住你的手問路。

他會跟隨你，向你微笑和交談，內心沒有一絲懷疑。

不要辜負他的信任，引導他到正路，並且祝福他。

把你的手按在他的頭上，為他祈求，雖然底下波濤洶湧，然而從天而降的風，會鼓起他的船帆，讓他航向平靜的天堂。

不要在匆忙中遺忘了他，讓他進到你的心裡，並且祝福他。

Benediction

Bless this little heart, this white soul that has won the kiss of heaven for our earth.

He loves the light of the sun, he loves the sight of his mother's face.

He has not learned to despise the dust, and to hanker after gold.

Clasp him to your heart and bless him.

He has come into this land of a hundred cross-roads.

I know not how he chose you from the crowd, came to your door, and grasped your hand to ask his way.

He will follow you, laughing and talking, and not a doubt in his heart.

Keep his trust, lead him straight and bless him.

Lay your hand on his head, and pray that though the waves underneath grow threatening, yet the breath from above may come and fill his sails and waft him to the haven of peace.

Forget him not in your hurry, let him come to your heart and bless him.

禮物／

我想送些東西給你，我的孩子，因為我們都漂泊在世界之河中。

我們的生命將被分開，我們之間的愛也將被遺忘。

但我沒有傻到希望用禮物來收買你的心。

你還年輕，還有很長的路，你把我們給你的愛一飲而盡，便轉身離去。

你有你的遊樂和玩伴。如果你沒有時間跟我們在一起，甚至不會想到我們，也就算了。

的確，我們在老年時，會有許多閒暇的時間，細數過去的日子，在心裡珍惜著已從手中永久離去的種種。

河流唱著歌曲飛快地流逝，衝破所有的堤防。但是山峰依舊聳立著，懷念著，充滿愛意地追隨著。

The Gift

I want to give you something, my child, for we are drifting in the stream of the world.

Our lives will be carried apart, and our love forgotten.

But I am not so foolish as to hope that I could buy your heart with my gifts.

Young is your life, your path long, and you drink the love we bring you at one draught and turn and run away from us.

You have your play and your playmates. What harm is there if you have no time or thought for us.

We, indeed, have leisure enough in old age to count the days that are past, to cherish in our hearts what our hands have lost for ever.

The river runs swift with a song, breaking through all barriers. But the mountain stays and remembers, and follows her with his love.

我的歌／

我的孩子，我這首歌將在你的身旁圍繞，如同熱戀中的雙臂。

我的這首歌將輕觸你的前額，如同祝福之吻。

當你一個人時，它將陪在你身旁，在你耳邊細語；當你在人群中，它將包圍你，使你超然物外。

我的歌將化為你的夢想之翼，把你的心送往未知的岸邊。

當黑夜遮蔽你的路途，它亦是緊緊追隨著你的不滅星光。

我的歌將進入你雙眸的瞳孔中，引領你直視萬物之心。

當我的聲音因死亡而沉寂時，我的歌仍將在你火熱的心中唱著。

My Song

This song of mine will wind its music around you, my child, like the fond arms of love.

This song of mine will touch your forehead like a kiss of blessing.

When you are alone it will sit by your side and whisper in your ear, when you are in the crowd it will fence you about with aloofness.

My song will be like a pair of wings to your dreams, it will transport your heart to the verge of the unknown.

It will be like the faithful star overhead when dark night is over your road.

My song will sit in the pupils of your eyes, and will carry your sight into the heart of things.

And when my voice is silent in death, my song will speak in your living heart.

孩子天使／

他們喧鬧爭鬥，他們懷疑失望，他們爭吵卻沒有結果。

我的孩子，讓你的生命到他們當中去，如一線光明，穩定而純潔，能讓他們喜悅而沉靜。

他們因貪心和妒忌而殘忍；他們的話語有如暗藏的刀，飢渴而嗜血。

我的孩子，去吧，去站在他們憤懣的心中，把你和善的目光望向他們，猶如向晚的寬容和平，讓日間的衝突得以止息。

我的孩子，讓他們看著你的臉，從而得知萬物的意義；讓他們愛你，進而讓他們彼此相愛。

我的孩子，來吧，坐在無垠的胸膛上。朝陽出來時，開放而且高舉你的心，像一朵盛開的花；夕陽落下時，低下你的頭，默默地完成這一天的禮拜。

The Child-Angel

They clamour and fight, they doubt and despair, they know no end to their wranglings.

Let your life come amongst them like a flame of light, my child, unflickering and pure, and delight them into silence.

They are cruel in their greed and their envy, their words are like hidden knives thirsting for blood.

Go and stand amidst their scowling hearts, my child, and let your gentle eyes fall upon them like the forgiving peace of the evening over the strife of the day.

Let them see your face, my child, and thus know the meaning of all things; let them love you and thus love each other.

Come and take your seat in the bosom of the limitless, my child. At sunrise open and raise your heart like a blossoming flower, and at sunset bend your head and in silence complete the worship of the day.

最後的買賣／

「來雇用我吧。」早晨，我邊喊邊走在石板路上。

皇帝坐著馬車，手裡拿著劍走來。

他拉著我的手，說道，「我要用權力來雇用你。」

但是他的權力對我而言不算什麼，於是他乘著馬車走了。

日正當中時，每間房子門戶緊閉。

我沿著彎曲的小巷走去。

一位老人帶著一袋金子走出來。

他斟酌了一下，說道：「我要用金錢來雇用你。」

他一塊一塊地數著，但我卻轉身離去了。

到了黃昏，花園的籬笆上開滿了花。

一位美人走出來，說道：「我要用微笑來雇用你。」

她的微笑黯淡了，化成淚水，她獨自走進黑暗中。

The Last Bargain

"Come and hire me," I cried, while in the morning I was walking on the stone-paved road.

Sword in hand, the King came in his chariot.

He held my hand and said, "I will hire you with my power."

But his power counted for nought, and he went away in his chariot.

In the heat of the midday the houses stood with shut doors.

I wandered along the crooked lane.

An old man came out with his bag of gold.

He pondered and said, "I will hire you with my money."

He weighed his coins one by one, but I turned away.

It was evening. The garden hedge was all aflower.

The fair maid came out and said, "I will hire you with a smile."

Her smile paled and melted into tears, and she went back alone into the dark.

太陽照耀在沙灘上，海波任性地浪花四濺。

一個小孩坐在那裡玩貝殼。

他抬起頭來，好像認識我似的，說道：「我不用東西雇你。」

從此以後，在孩子的遊戲中成交的買賣，讓我得以自由。

The sun glistened on the sand, and the sea waves broke waywardly.

A child sat playing with shells.

He raised his head and seemed to know me, and said, "I hire you with nothing."

From thenceforward that bargain struck in child's play made me a free man.

關於作者

羅賓德拉納德‧泰戈爾（Rabindranath Tagore, 1861-1941）是一位享譽世界的印度詩人、小說家、藝術家、思想家與社會活動家，是第一位獲得諾貝爾文學獎的亞洲人，一生寫了 50 多部詩集，被稱為「詩聖」。

他出生在印度一個富有哲學與文學修養的貴族家庭，8 歲就開始寫詩，13 歲便能對長詩與頌歌體詩集進行創作，展現出其非凡的文學天賦。1913 年他因自譯的英文版《吉檀迦利》榮獲諾貝爾文學獎，自此躋身於世界文壇。

他的作品具有極高的歷史、藝術價值，深受民眾喜愛。其主要詩作有不少被世人廣知，如《新月集》、《吉檀迦利》、《漂鳥集》、《採果集》、《園丁集》等。除了諸多詩集外，還創作了 12 部中長篇小說，100 多部短篇小說，20 多部劇本以及大量的文學、哲學、政治論著，並在 70 歲時開始學習繪畫，此外還創作了數量繁多的各類歌曲，影響後世甚鉅。

關於作品

《新月集》創作於 1903 年，是泰戈爾的代表作之一。以描繪孩子們的遊戲和童趣的方式，巧妙地把孩子們純潔與奇特活潑的思維方式展現給世人。泰戈爾在詩集中所想要謳歌的便是人的一生中最為寶貴的心性：童真。

除了描繪孩童的純真，詩中還極力讚美母愛。正如現實當中缺少母愛的孩子很難體會到幸福是什麼一樣，他深諳個中哲理，在作品中融合這兩種截然不同、卻緊緊相繫的事物，給予了讚頌。詩集問世之後，泰戈爾還因此被譽為「兒童詩人」。

每首詩都彷彿有著無法抗拒的魔力，把我們從罪惡貪婪、黑暗的世道中牽引到純潔天真的孩童世界，不僅勾起我們對童年純粹美好的生活回憶，還剪去在現實困境裡掙扎的人們心中陰暗的一隅，淨化心靈、陶冶性情。

關於譯者

鄭振鐸（1898-1958），著名文學家、作家、翻譯家和文物考古學家，同時也是新文化和新文學運動的宣導者。

他在1922年和1923年兩年間翻譯出版了泰戈爾的《漂鳥集》與《新月集》，從此便開始系統、大量地對泰戈爾的詩歌進行翻譯。這些譯作對當時的文壇產生了重要影響，亦促進中國新文學與西洋文學的交流。

因鄭振鐸主要翻譯的是泰戈爾的詩歌及印度古代的寓言，在他逝世後，印度的著名學者海曼歌·比斯瓦斯在1958年《悼念鄭振鐸》一文中寫道：「他可能是第一個把印度古典文學和現代文學介紹給中國讀者的人，他同樣是當前中印文化交流的先驅。」海曼歌·比斯瓦斯對鄭振鐸在印度文化方面的翻譯貢獻給予了很高的評價。

泰戈爾生平年表

1861	0	5 月 7 日，羅賓德拉納特·泰戈爾出生於孟加拉加爾各答市的喬拉桑格，為家中十四子。
1869	8	開始練習寫詩。
1874	13	被錄取至聖澤維爾學校。
1875	14	母親去世。在《甘露市場報》上發表愛國詩篇；發表長篇敘事詩《野花》。離開聖澤維爾學校。
1877	16	發表第一篇短篇小說《女乞丐》以及敘事詩《詩人的故事》
1878	17	赴英國留學。於《婆羅蒂》雜誌上連載《旅歐書札》。
1880	19	從英國返回印度。
1881	20	發表音樂劇《蟻垤仙人的天才》。1882 年出版《暮歌集》。於《婆羅蒂》連載長篇歷史小說《皇后市場》。發表詩劇《破碎的心》。雜文集《雜論》出版。
1882	21	開始創作《晨歌集》並於 1883 年出版。
1883	22	與穆里納莉妮·黛維結婚。
1884	23	擔任「梵社」秘書。發表歌劇《大自然的報復》。發表詩集《畫與歌集》、《帕努辛赫詩抄》。發表短篇小說《河邊的台階》。
1885	24	創作長篇歷史小說《賢哲王》。12 月，國大黨

		成立。
1886	25	長女瑪圖莉萊達出生，詩集《剛與柔》出版。
1888	27	長子羅提德拉納特出生。
1889	28	寫出無韻詩體劇本《國王和皇后》
1890	29	離開孟買，前往義大利、英國和法國旅行。次女蕾努卡出生。詩集《心靈集》出版。將《賢哲王》改編成詩劇，題名為《犧牲》上演。
1891	30	開始持續創作《郵政局長》、《還債》…等短篇小說。與侄子蘇倫創辦文學月刊《實踐》，直到 1895 年停刊。發表遊記《旅歐日記》。
1892	31	發表詩劇《齊德拉》，並於 1936 年改編成舞劇。短篇小說《摩訶摩耶》，《喀布爾人》發表。
1893	32	短篇小說《棄絕》和《素芭》等發表。
1894	33	小兒子索明德拉納特出生。擔任孟加拉文學協會副主席。出版短篇小說集《小說匯編》一、二集、《太陽和烏雲》。詩集《金色船集》出版。發表詩劇《離別時的詛咒》。
1895	34	創作短篇小說《飢餓的石頭》，與侄子蘇倫德羅納特合創黃麻經營企業。
1896	35	詩集《江河集》、《繽紛集》、《收穫集》出版。創作詩劇《瑪麗妮》。
1898	37	主編《婆羅蒂》雜誌。英國政府通過「反煽動法」，在加爾各答群眾集會上發表名為《窒息》的演說，嚴厲譴責英國殖民當局對民族主義運

		動領袖提拉克的迫害。
1899	38	加爾各答流行鼠疫，協助救治患者。侄子波朗德拉納特去世。創辦的企業倒閉。發表短詩集《塵埃集》。
1900	39	出版詩集《故事詩集》、《故事集》、《剎那集》和《幻想集》。
1901	40	在聖蒂尼克坦成立梵學書院。任《孟加拉觀察》雜誌編輯，直至 1906 年止。於該雜誌連載長篇小說《眼中沙》。詩集《祭品集》出版。
1902	41	辦學因經濟困難，典賣土地和妻子的首飾。11 月 23 日妻子病逝，寫哀悼詩，1903 年結集出版，題為《懷念集》。
1903	42	二女蕾努卡病逝。出版詩集《兒童集》。於《孟加拉觀察》連載長篇小說《沈船》。
1905	44	1 月 15 日，父親於加爾各答逝世。創辦政治性月刊《寶庫》。積極參與反對殖民主義愛國運動。創作現為孟加拉國國歌的《金色的孟加拉》等大量愛國歌曲。
1906	45	送長子羅提德拉納特到美國學習農業科學。出版《沈船》單行本，發表詩集《渡口集》。
1907	46	於《外鄉人》上連載長篇小說《戈拉》。回聖蒂尼克坦從事文學創作與教育活動。發表論文《疾病與治療》。出版散文集《五彩繽紛》和《膜拜品德》，論文集《古代文學》、《民間文學》、《文學》、《現代文學》，劇本《滑稽劇本集》，

		雜文集《幽默》。小兒子去世。
1908	47	主持孟加拉邦政治協商會議。發表論文集《國王和人民》、《集體》、《社會》、《教育》和《自治》。發表詩集《故事和敘事集》、《致敬集》。出版詩劇《秋天的節日》和散文劇《皇冠》。
1909	48	長子羅提德拉納特離美回國。發表劇本《懺悔》。出版宗教、哲學演講集《聖蒂尼克坦》1-8集。
1910	49	孟加拉語詩集《吉檀迦利》出版。長篇小說《戈拉》出版。散文劇本《暗室之王》發表。於《外鄉人》上連載《回憶錄》，1912 年出版單行本。編寫劇本《郵局》，1912 年發表。創作歌曲《人民的意志》，1950 年 1 月 24 日成為印度國歌。演講集《聖蒂尼克坦》12-13 集出版。
1912	51	孟加拉文學協會為他舉辦慶祝會。5 月 27 日，動身前往英、美國，直至第二年 9 月 4 日返回印度。詩集《吉檀迦利》英譯版出版。
1913	52	英文詩集《吉檀迦利》出版獲得諾貝爾文學獎。加爾各答大學授予名譽文學博士學位。英文詩集《園丁集》、《新月集》出版。
1914	53	發表短篇小說《一個女人的信》。
1915	54	甘地訪問聖蒂尼克坦，泰戈爾會見甘地。獲英皇授予爵士榮銜。演講集《聖蒂尼克坦》14 集出版，第二年出版 15-17 集。

1916	55	到訪日本和美國分別發表題為《國家主義》、《人格》等演說。長篇小說《家庭與世界》和《四個人》出版。發表詩集《鴻雁》與英文詩集《採果集》和《漂鳥集》。劇本《春之循環》和短篇小集《小說七篇》出版。
1917	56	於加爾各答的印度國大黨會議上宣讀詩篇《印度的祈禱》。
1918	57	大女兒去世。詩集《遁逃集》出版。
1919	58	憤怒抗議英國殖民當局在阿姆利則槍殺無辜群眾，宣佈放棄英國政府授予爵士稱號。發表遊記《訪日散記》。
1920	59	前往英國、法國、荷蘭和美國。為國際大學募捐。短篇小說集《第二個》出版。
1921	60	3 月回國歸途中經英國又到法國，之後訪問德國、丹麥、瑞典、奧地利等國。於巴黎會見羅曼·羅蘭。在德國會見托馬斯·曼。7 月回印度。12 月 23 日國際大學正式成立，將聖蒂尼克坦的財產捐給國際大學。劇本《還債》出版。英譯本《沈船》、英文本《游思集》出版。
1922	61	訪問南印度和錫蘭（今斯里蘭卡），在可倫坡和加勒舉行了一系列講座。12 月長兄去世。創作散文詩集《隨想集》。發表象徵劇《摩克多塔拉》。出版兒童詩集《童年的濕婆集》。
1923	62	將已發表著作的版權交付國際大學。《國際大學》季刊、英文版《戈拉》出版。參與劇目《犧

		牲》的演出。發表音樂劇《春天》。
1924	63	於加爾各答大學發表文學主題演講。訪問中國，在上海、濟南、北京等地發表演說，會見梅蘭芳等知名藝文界人士，並與末代皇帝溥儀會面。訪問日本後回國。應邀訪問秘魯。創作《西行日記》和詩作《普爾比集》。
1925	64	1 月離開布宜諾斯艾利斯前往義大利等地。2 月回國。5 月泰戈爾於聖蒂尼克坦會見甘地，但對不合作運動有著不同看法。年底，被選為印度哲學大會主席。
1926	65	於達卡大學發表演說。再次應邀出國，訪問義大利、英國、挪威、奧地利、瑞典、丹麥、德國、捷克、南斯拉夫、羅馬尼亞、匈牙利、保加利亞、希臘再經埃及回國。出版詩作《隨感集》；發表劇本《舞女的膜拜》、《獨身者協會》、《南迪妮》、《報復心理》、《最後一場雨》。
1927	66	著手創作長篇小說《糾纏》。在巴拉特普爾主持印地文學會議。發表劇本《舞王》。訪問馬來西亞、印尼和泰國。於《千姿百態》雜誌上連載《爪哇通訊》。
1928	67	與印度著名政治活動家、哲學家奧羅賓多會面。訪問錫蘭（今斯里蘭卡）和班加羅爾。發表劇本《最後的拯救》。創作長篇小說《最後的詩篇》。

1929	68	訪問加拿大、日本和南西貢。發表詩集書信集《旅行者》。
1930	69	出訪法國、英國、德國、瑞士、俄國、美國，並於上述的一些國家舉辦畫展。在英國牛津大學發表主題為《人的宗教》的演講。開始在《僑民》雜誌發表《俄國書簡》，1931 年集結出版。
1931	70	在印度市政大廳隆重慶祝 70 大壽。發表劇本《新穎》和《擺脫詛咒》。出版詩集《聚寶集》，《森林之聲集》和《通俗讀物集》。《泰戈爾全集》出版。
1932	71	抗議英國殖民當局逮捕甘地。出訪伊朗和伊拉克。唯一的孫子去世。出版詩集《再次集》和《總結集》，劇本《時間的流逝》發表。英文詩集《金色之書》出版。
1933	72	於加爾各答發表印度啟蒙主義先驅羅姆·摩罕的演說，在安得拉大學以《人》為題發表演講。詩集《五彩集》發表。劇本《紙牌王國》、《不可接觸的姑娘》和《竹笛》發表。中篇小說《兩姐妹》發表。
1934	73	率領國際大學業餘舞劇團前往錫蘭（今斯里蘭卡）和南印度巡迴演出。
1935	74	走訪北印度，並在幾所大學發表演說，為國際大學募籌資金。發表詩集《最後的星期集》和《小徑集》。英文論文集《東方和西方》出版。《泰戈爾歌曲二十六首》出版。

1936	75	在加爾各答針對教育問題發表演講。英文論文集《使教育符合國情》發表。詩集《葉盤集》和《黑牛集》出版。遊記《瀛洲遊記》出版。論文集《文學的道路》和《韻律》出版。
1937	76	在加爾各答大學以孟加拉語發表演說。在聖蒂尼克坦主持國際大學中國學院成立典禮。著文《印度和中國》。出版詩集《非洲集》、《錯位集》和《兒歌之畫集》。短篇小說集《他》出版。
1938	77	寫信給日本詩人野口米次郎，譴責日本帝國主義侵略中國的罪行。詩集《晚祭集》和《邊緣集》出版。
1939	78	詩集《戲謔集》、《天燈集》出版。發表舞劇《解放》和《薩瑪》。
1940	79	泰戈爾在聖蒂尼克坦最後一次會見甘地。牛津大學授予泰戈爾博士學位。病情轉劇，被送往加爾各答就醫。英文自傳《我的童年》出版。詩集《新生集》、《嗩吶集》、《病榻集》出版。短篇小說集《三個同伴》出版。
1941	80	4 月發表公開演說，題為《文明的危機》。7 月病情惡化在加爾各答動手術。8 月 7 日在加爾各答祖居與世長辭。詩集《康復集》、《生辰集》、《兒歌集》和《最後的作品集》等出版。

新月集/泰戈爾著; 鄭振鐸譯. -- 初版. --
臺北市：笛藤, 2017.10
面；公分. --（世界經典文學）
中英對照雙語版
ISBN 978-957-710-706-0（平裝）
867.51 106016388

2019年7月26日 初版第2刷 定價260元

著者 泰戈爾 Rabindranath Tagore
譯者 鄭振鐸
審譯 陳珮馨
封面設計 王舒玗
內頁設計 王舒玗
總編輯 賴巧凌
發行所 笛藤出版圖書有限公司
發行人 林建仲
地址 台北市中山區長安東路二段171號3樓3室
電話 (02)2777-3682
傳真 (02)2777-3672
總經銷 聯合發行股份有限公司
地址 新北市新店區寶橋路235巷6弄6號2樓
電話 (02)2917-8022・(02)2917-8042
製版廠 造極彩色印刷製版股份有限公司
地址 新北市中和區中山路2段340巷36號
電話 (02)2240-0333・(02)2248-3904
劃撥帳戶 八方出版股份有限公司
劃撥帳號 19809050

新月集／泰戈爾詩選
中英對照雙語版

The Crescent Moon